Grandma is..... Seven Days a Week

YVONNE S.
AND
SARAH Y. LEE

Grandma is… Seven Days a Week
Copyright © 2021 by Yvonne S. and Sarah Y. Lee

First Edition

Hardcover ISBN: 978-1-68515-107-2
Paperback ISBN: 978-1-68515-108-9
eBook ISBN: 978-1-68515-109-6

DEDICATION

Mom,
I dedicate this book to you.
When we started writing it, I felt like I was two.

Wishing you were here to help complete your vision.
No worries… I know it was your time, and now it's MY
time to carry the sword to complete our mission.

The love you gave Leah as a grandmother was so
amazing. She misses you so much, I believe she puts
her emotions in her dancing.

Knowing you are smiling and looking down from
the stars. Publishing this book,
is just the beginning!

Your daughter,
Sarah

My Grandma is a very *special* person. She has always been that way.

On *Sunday*, I needed something extra, and Grandma was there to save the day!

My Grandma is a very *considerate* person. She has always been that way.

On *Monday*, I wanted something sweet to eat, and so she put cookies and milk on my favorite blue tray.

My Grandma is a very *talkative* person. She has always been that way.

On *Tuesday*, I called her on the telephone. She talked, I talked, we talked … until there was nothing more to say.

My Grandma is a very *under-standing* person. She has always been that way.

On *Wednesday*, I broke her pretty vase. Later, she let me help her make another one by using clay.

My Grandma is a very *smart* person. She has always been that way.

On *Thursday*, I showed her what my teacher taught today. She took the chalkboard out and showed me a better way.

My Grandma is a very *funny* person. She has always been that way.

On *Friday*, she told me many funny jokes until (oops!), she had to get me the spray!

My Grandma is a very *loving* person. She has always been that way.

On *Saturday*, I needed a hug and a kiss, and she gave those to me right away!

My Grandma was one of a kind. She had always been that way.Seven days a week, she loved me.... And I wish she was still here to play!

ABOUT THE AUTHOR

Sarah Lee is an only child, born and raised in Baltimore, Maryland. She earned a BA in psychology from Delaware State University and an MA in special education from Grand Canyon University. She has worked in the Baltimore City Schools in the area of special education for over 20 years. Teaching was not her first career choice. Her mom, Yvonne Lee, inspired Sarah to stay in education. Yvonne was also with the Baltimore City Schools for over 33 years and loved her job. She worked with the special education department as well as the preschool department. Yvonne started writing this book in a little spiral notebook in the early 1980s, reading for Sarah what she had written, and then asking her to help fill in the blanks. In 2009, Sarah had a daughter named Leah. The birth of Yvonne's granddaughter was everything. Leah gave more meaning to Yvonne's life. Since Yvonne's passing in 2019, Sarah has wanted to find ways to keep her spirit alive. Finding this book was a blessing!

CPSIA information can be obtained
at www.ICGtesting.com
Printed in the USA
LVHW071535240222
711930LV00008B/522

9 781685 151072